MW00875405

THE CHRISTMAS MAN

A Short Story

by

Joseph Metcalfe

Cover design by Brooke Metcalfe

Copyright © 2014 Joseph Metcalfe

All Rights Reserved

ISBN-13:

978-1505398045

ISBN-10:

1505398045

*To my wife, Brooke, and our beautiful children,
Aidan, Jude and Charlotte,*

You each fill my days with awe and enchantment.

*We all share one big wish for the future.
Believe that it will come true!*

THE CHRISTMAS MAN

Contents

1. The Perfect Village

If you've ever felt the excitement before Christmas, you know, that kind of feeling where it seems impossible to fall asleep at bedtime because your tummy tickles itself from the inside, then I think you need to know why that feeling comes at such a special time of the year. It started a long time ago in a small, remote village in a very far away land on the day that winter officially begins in the northern world.

It was a particularly harsh start to the season for the people in the village, not just because of the cold winter where the frosty ground would make your toes feel like icicles but because they were not very wealthy, in fact not at all. Every family would live in a very small house with only one room which served as the kitchen, living room and bedroom all at the same time. The bathroom was more like a small shed in the back garden and the icy wind would easily blow through the cracks in the walls making bath time even less enjoyable than it already was.

The date was December 21st and down at the village's very small market square people came out to see what the few sellers had to sell. Even though they didn't really have enough money to buy anything it was still a good place to come and meet their fellow villagers and grumble about how poor they were. However, something very unusual happened that nobody expected, especially at this time of year. A curious man, with no shoes or socks, a thin pair of trousers, a worn out shirt and a strange hat wandered into the market square carrying a bag in his hand.

The villagers stopped in their conversations and the square fell silent as everyone stared at the unexpected visitor. The man took off his hat and asked, "Can you spare any food or money for the poor?"

Now this takes a lot of courage to ask especially when everyone is looking at you and the people themselves have just been talking about how poor they are. The most important thing if you are a beggar in this situation is to make sure that the first person you ask is the type of person who will at least give you something so that everybody else might do the same. Unfortunately for this man, the first person to respond said, "No. I'm too poor to help. Sorry!"

As the man went around one by one to each person who was present in the village square everybody gave the same answer until he reached the very last person, who also rejected his plea. Now that everyone had refused his petition he turned to all the people and asked, "Even though you have nothing to offer me, it is very far to the next village so may I please have permission to stay in your village?"

The people were reluctant at first to let him stay in fear that he'd not only want to lodge in one of their small houses but also that he'd only be back begging for food and money again the next day. Sensing this reluctancy he continued, "I'll gather some fire wood together and sleep at the edge of the village so as not to disturb anyone, if that will be less trouble for you."

The people spoke in soft voices to each other until one man finally announced that the villagers had agreed to his request. The beggar man smiled and said, "This village is perfect. Thank you!" And with that he put his hat back on, reached into his bag and turned it inside out. Instead of it revealing any contents, the bag itself unfolded into a very warm and expensive looking coat. He put it on and wandered up to the edge of the village where he started to gather firewood.

The appearance of the coat had the people both wary and intrigued for if he was hiding a big coat to try to win their pity then perhaps he couldn't be trusted. On the other hand, how had he managed to obtain such a beautiful coat?

While the people mingled and discussed their new subject for the rest of the day, the man gathered firewood at the top of road that lead into the village. His pile of wood was quite substantial and he soon found that he likely had enough for a nice fire that would last for several days. As the day drew gradually nearer to it's end and the darkness of the early night was being painted into the sky the villagers started to return to their houses.

Candles were being lit inside people's homes and placed on the window sills to give light to both the houses and the street. The man, who had not even started his fire yet, gave a smile over the village and was at peace with where he found himself. In fact he found himself getting excited. Very excited, in fact. So much so that he didn't know if he was going to be able to sleep at all that night.

As the evening was getting colder the man knelt down by one of the stacks of wood, reached into his pocket and pulled out a beautiful, softly roaring flame that he placed on the stack of wood so that it instantly turned into a well established fire. He then sat next to the fire, reached into his pocket and pulled out a pencil and a quite large piece of paper and started to draw.

2. A Boy And His Brother

The next morning the people woke up to yet another cold but sunny day and had practically forgotten about the beggar man, let alone wonder if he had survived the brisk night's air. After they had finished their meager breakfasts and had folded up their blankets into a pile in the corner of their homes they all trundled off to the market square to have another grumble about how they couldn't afford anything due to their poverty.

After a few minutes of the usual discussion someone remembered the beggar man and finally questioned if anyone had seen him. They all turned to look towards where he had gathered firewood and at first didn't see anything. Not because there was nothing to see, but because what they were looking at was so immense, so huge and overwhelming that they simply couldn't see it at first. But once they actually saw it, their jaws fell wide open all at the same time and you could hear one giant group gasp.

The fire was no longer just a fire. Around it now stood a huge chimney, that extended through a very steep, green roof, that itself was at least twenty times higher than the tallest building in the village. Supporting the chimney were immense walls with magnificent crystal cut windows divided up by thin strips of lead into little diamond shape panes. In the middle of the wall stood the most magnificent wooden doors that seemed so large that you would need twenty strong men to open just one of them. The building extended back so far that it appeared that you could fit the entire village inside and still have room left over. But most glorious of all were the majestic golden gates that would lead into the big courtyard in front of this magnificent mansion and whose radiant glow cast an incredible warm hue over the village.

As the people stared at the building, one of the huge front doors opened ever so slightly and the silhouette of the man came up to the front gates. When he opened the gates the sun's reflection upon them made a golden light that moved over the village. As the people watched with stunned looks on their faces he walked down to where they were gathered.

With a huge smile on his face he asked, "Did you all sleep deeply last night?"

Strangely, nobody had mentioned it until this point, but yes, in fact, they had all fallen asleep quite deeply and had enjoyed one of their best night of sleep for a long time. So deep asleep that they didn't even hear a single bit of construction on the man's mansion. For the second time in two days the market square had fallen silent. Even the birds had stopped chirping in anticipation of what would happen next.

The man was dressed differently apart from his very expensive looking coat that looked like it would take three of the richest families in the village a whole year to save up to buy. He now wore a fluffy, warm, matching scarf around his neck, a matching hat that would keep you as warm as a fireplace would, a pair of very smart trousers and a pair of beautifully polished very cozy looking boots.

He gazed around as if he was looking at each man, woman and child directly in the eye and then that huge grin grew over his face, "Who would like a sweetie?" he announced in a clear, inviting and friendly manner.

At first no one moved, probably because they were mystified by this whole new event. Slowly the children started to look up at their mums and dads as if to ask if it was OK to go up to the man. Most of the parents put their hand on their children's shoulders to prevent them from running up. But for one little boy, whose parents were watching very closely, he had no fear and started walking toward the man. The little boy was shivering, not from nervousness, but because he didn't have a coat to wear, just a sweater that had a hole in the elbow.

As the boy reached the man he looked up and said, "Please may I have a sweetie?"

The man looked down at the boy and asked, "What flavor would you like?"

The little boy's mouth dropped wide open as he had never been given a choice before. His family were so poor that he had only ever had three sweets and one piece of chocolate in his whole life.

"What flavor do you have?" replied the boy.

"Name any flavor you could imagine," invited the man.

The little boy thought for a minute and said, "Strawberry?"

The man grimaced a little before announcing, "That's an easy one! Strawberry it is."

He then reached into his pocket and pulled out a sweet whose wrapper looked exactly like a strawberry. The little boy hesitated as he didn't want to remove the wrapper because of how fine it looked.

"Go ahead. Eat it!" ordered the man in a very kind way.

The little boy carefully removed the wrapper and put the sweet into his mouth. Everybody was now staring at the little boy. The instant the sweet touched his tongue it was very clear to see that this was the nicest thing he had ever tasted in his whole life. He looked as if he was eating an entire strawberry field of the most delicious strawberries the world had ever grown and the look on his face was as if he was floating in the clouds.

As much as he wanted the sweet to last forever it was eventually gone and the man smiled at the little boy before announcing, "Anyone else?"

Still nobody moved, except for shivering, which they had forgotten they were doing with the unexpected events of the day.

"Well, as nobody else wants a sweet, would you like another one?" he asked the boy.

"Another one? Oh, yes please! I can give it to my brother," proclaimed the small child.

"To your brother? How thoughtful! Then perhaps I shall give you two more. One for you and one for him, though how about something different this time?" the man offered. "Think of anything you want."

"Do you have any chocolate?" asked the boy.

"Well, of course I do. But what type of chocolate?" smiled the man.

"Um, I didn't know you could have different types of chocolate, good sir."

"Then try hard to imagine. What flavor would go well with chocolate?" pressed the man.

The little boy closed his eyes and thought really hard as he tried to remember the flavor of chocolate. It just so happened that besides strawberry, the other two flavors of sweets he had tasted were a toffee candy and a mint. "How about toffee chocolate?"

"Excellent suggestion young man, toffee chocolate it is. But may I have your permission to make it a toffee HOT chocolate flavor sweetie?" inquired the man as he raised an eyebrow.

"Hot chocolate? I've heard of it, but never had it before. Will it burn my tongue?"

The man gave a reassuring smile and reached into his pocket and pulled out two golden brown wrappers, "Here you go, try this!"

The little boy raced back to his brother and the two boys eagerly unwrapped their sweets.

The villagers were now wishing that they could swap places with the young boys as they keenly awaited their reaction. Moments after they popped the sweets into their mouths everyone could see that the boys' shivering gradually stopped with every chew.

"It's delicious," exclaimed the boy.

"And warm," added his brother.

"And it's like I'm drinking the most delicious..."

Neither of the boys could speak another word, so luscious was the sweet taste of toffee hot chocolate.

Everyone was now poised as they waited for just one more invitation, but the offer would not come.

"Well," exclaimed the owner of the immense building, "lovely to see you again. Good day to you all." And with that he turned and walked back up the path toward his glorious residence.

The villagers were stunned and it wasn't long until the young boys were surrounded by questioning neighbors who were begging to find out just how good the sweets really were. The golden reflection glimmered once again across the market as the gates to the mansion closed and the man disappeared inside. Remarkably, the two boys didn't feel cold again for the rest of the day.

As the market drew to is close, with nobody buying or selling anything, the man peered through one of the crystal windows and smiled at the village and started to get that very excited feeling again. He knew he was going to be in for a big night once again. Seeing that all the villagers had gone home for the night he grabbed his lovely big coat, his warm boots, scarf and hat and set off to walk through the village.

3. Golden Numbers

The first thing he noticed was that none of the houses were very different from each other. The village didn't have street names and the houses didn't have numbers on them. Everybody just knew whose house was whose and which house was which. As he passed each house he peered into the window of the house to learn about every single family.

Most families were huddled together around a fireplace, trying to keep warm while the mother of the family prepared a meager hot soup over the fire for dinner. Some families read stories or told jokes to each other, some sat quietly and stared while other families sang songs. Although he loved to hear the stories the man particularly enjoyed the laughter and the singing.

As he observed each family he would reach into his pocket, pull out a parchment, a pot of ink that had no lid and a long feather so he could write a note for himself to record his thoughts. Before he left each house, he would reach into his other pocket, pull out a paintbrush and a pot of paint made of pure gold that glowed by itself without the need for light and decorated the door post with a number.

The next morning was the day before the day before Christmas. Usually this was the most exciting day of the year for gift givers as it was the day everyone would go and buy their presents and gifts for each other and the market sellers would sell all their goods. However, everybody knew that this Christmas would be different as there wasn't spare money left over for presents. Everyone was preparing what they were going to grumble about at the market but no such conversation ever took place.

As each family left their house, they couldn't help but notice the glowing number that so beautifully decorated their door frames. Its glow was so stunning that all thoughts of grumbling simply disappeared. Even if they thought that they would grumble about the fact someone had painted it on their door frames without permission the thought would soon vanish from their minds.

Once each family arrived at the market square they would all be comparing what number they each had and even though they were all decorated with the same paint, they all had a unique style of decor, none more beautiful than the other. The market sellers didn't even remember to set up their stalls. Instead they all trundled from house to house to examine their new numbers. Nobody had ever counted before, but now everyone knew that there were 152 houses in the village.

When the day was over, nobody actually left when the sun went down. The twinkling glow from the numbers was now a little bit brighter than the night before and people stayed together to tell their stories and sing songs to each other. The man looked out of his house and smiled. This village was perfect.

He reached for his big jacket and turned it inside out, put it on and left his house through a side gate so that people wouldn't become distracted by the big gates opening. The reason he wore his jacket inside out was in fact because his jacket was truly enchanted. When worn the right way around, people would see that it was a magnificent coat and everyone would notice it. When worn inside out people simply wouldn't notice and thus wouldn't see the man. It's not that it turned him invisible. It just stopped people from noticing.

As the man walked unnoticed through the villagers he stopped to enjoy the festivities, listen to the same stories being recounted again and again, laughed at the same jokes and hummed along with the all too familiar tunes. It didn't take long until some of the younger children started asking their parents for food and it seemed that the families would all have to go home soon. Not wanting to change the happiness that filled the market square the man reached into his pocket and pulled out a little piece of wood.

Taking the wood in his hands he stretched it out, just like a baker would stretch his dough, and molded the wood into a very long table with benches along each side. It was almost like watching a finely skilled potter working with clay, except in this instance the clay was wood. Having completed the table, he reached once again into his pocket and pulled out a giant table cloth and unrolled it onto the table with one big flick of the wrist.

This table cloth wasn't only made of the finest fabric these people had ever seen. It was also filled with gorgeous colored plates that seemed to have little twinkling lights inside them that fell exactly into place. As they landed they would make sounds of tiny bells, each plate tuned to a different pitch so that they chimed glorious tunes as they came to rest on the table. No sooner than the plates had landed on the table cloth, a bowl also fell on top of the plate and golden knives, forks and spoons landed in perfect position around them, continuing the melody. The table looked set for the banquet of a king. A very fun king!

Though no one noticed the man they certainly noticed the table and gathered around in astonishment. Nobody had any thoughts of going home now. The children were giggly with excitement and their parents were in awe. Nobody had ever seen anything quite like this before.

While the people were distracted by the appearance of the table, the man walked a little way away and reached once more into his pocket and pulled out a frame that consisted of two triangles at each end and a long metal pole that would connect the triangles together. He then put his hand deep into his pocket and pulled out a delicious piece of beef that slid right on to the metal pole. Next a very large soup pot emerged from his coat, filled with the freshest of delumptious vegetables and potatoes in an exquisite broth and was placed under the meat. Now that everything was set, he reached into his pocket once again and pulled out a flame that he placed under the pot. In a single puff of fire, the meat was cooked, dripping it's deliciousness into to the soup pot which filled the market square with it's incredible aroma.

Though the villagers might have thought nothing would have distracted them from the attention they were giving to the table and it's wares, none could resist turning to look at the blast of fire that was soon followed by the mouth watering scents that filled their nostrils. There was no holding back. One by one they each grabbed their plates and bowls and lined up on both sides, piling their plates with pulled strips of beef and filling their bowls with stew.

By the time they returned to their places at the table warm, freshly baked rolls with fluffy butter and multi-colored crystal glasses, topped almost to the top with fizzy, sweet drinks, had appeared at every place setting. And nobody had noticed who had put them there.

The people had been so hungry that they probably didn't realize just how hungry they were. They also didn't notice the man who was sitting among them, not only enjoying the feast himself, but enjoying the delightful feeling among the villagers even more than he was enjoying the food. By the time everyone was filled to the brim, there wasn't a single scrap of food left over, not a crumb to spare and not a drop of drink unfinished. The villagers started their singing again and the man quietly slipped away, unnoticed. When he reached his house he looked back at the market square and thought to himself, "This village is perfect!"

4. Notes On The Tree

The next morning the sun rose above the horizon, but not a soul stirred. Everyone was so deep asleep with full bellies and happy dreams that they forgot to wake up when the sun rose. When they finally did awaken nobody thought about being poor. They were all remarkably happy. A few of the villagers gathered back at the market square expecting to see the table, but it was gone. There were no signs whatsoever of the festivities of the night before.

Almost 20 people had now arrived at the village square and started to discuss the events that had taken place in their village in the past few days and of course their conversation turned back to the arrival of the beggar man who now lived in the huge mansion that overlooked the village. They decided it was time to go and speak with him. As they were about to leave, one of the small children shouted out, "Look! Someone has planted a small tree."

Everybody gathered around to examine the new discovery. Sure enough, right where the table had stood the night before was a very small fir tree with a small tag with a hand written note attached to the top. It read, "Please pull me up." How they hadn't noticed it before was a complete mystery but then again, a lot of very unusual things were happening in this village and the 'unusual' was becoming very normal.

What did it mean by, 'Please pull me up'? The tree was already standing and its roots were planted firmly in the cold, hard ground beneath.

"Perhaps it means to dig it up," declared one of the men.

"Nonsense!" cried another man, "this ground would break your shovel if you tried to dig in it."

The little child who found it added, "or perhaps it just means..." and with that she pulled the tag upwards. No sooner had she done that the tree sprang up another three feet and as it did, half a dozen more branches popped out of the trunk, each with a little ribbon attached to the end and another note appeared. This time is said, "Pull these ribbons at exactly the same time, but no matter what DON'T LET GO!"

The villagers were incredibly intrigued by what might happen next and it didn't take long for six people to step forward and grab a piece of ribbon. One of the women who was standing by said, "On the count of three, everybody pull. 1, 2, 3!"

As they pulled the ribbons the tree raised out of the ground another few feet and just like before, nine new branches launched out of the trunk, though this time they were a little bit longer which meant everyone had to stand back a little bit. A new note was attached to one of the branches which read, "Same rules apply!" Seconds later fifteen people held a ribbon and another count was given and as they all pulled the same thing happened. The tree raised up a few feet, new branches emerged and a new note said, "I think you had better go and get all of the villagers. Leave nobody at home! Just don't let the two boys who ate sweets take hold of a ribbon. It is forbidden!"

A couple of the older boys who had witnessed what had happened started racing back to the houses, knocking on doors and shouting, "Come to the market square now! It's urgent!" The message spread faster than the boys could run and within twenty minutes, every villager was in the center of the square in wonderment of what was going on. Each time they pulled their ribbons together the tree raised up, popping out new longer branches with ribbons attached, each ribbon that had previously been pulled got longer and bystanders each stepped up to take hold of another newly formed ribbon.

Occasionally, reminder notes to 'not let go, NO MATTER WHAT,' would appear and once or twice they didn't pull all at the same time, which meant nothing happened until they got it right. Eventually every man, woman and child had hold of a ribbon, except for the two boys who had been given sweets from the beggar. Even they felt as incredibly excited as everyone else, although it would be truthful to say there was a little disappointed too that they hadn't been involved.

The tree itself was immense. It was taller even than the chimney of the beggar's house, but so vibrant was the curiosity of the people that they never even thought to stop once it reached a certain height. It did look truly magnificent with over six hundred ribbons hanging off the tips of every branch, nobody daring to let go.

As every villager, except the two boys, pulled their ribbons the tree raised up one more time only this time just two new, very small branches appeared and of course a note was attached to a ring that was dangling from one of them.

"To the last remaining boys, please make sure that everyone holds on to their ribbons, no matter what, and then pull this ring."

The brother of the boy who received the first sweet, stepped up and grabbed hold of the ring and, after having reassured everyone to hold on to their ribbons, gave a mighty pull to the ring. The cord the ring was attached to snapped in half and the boy fell onto his back. It was a good job that he did, for at the very moment the cord broke the tree lifted up off the ground and started to spin.

With everyone holding firm to their ribbons the tree started to wrap itself in the beautiful silk ribbons, some of which started to dissolve into a colorful melange of sparkling dust that spewed out clouds of glittering rain that soon formed back together into a glowing tinsel. Some of the ribbons pulled out giant crystal balls that appeared to change color depending upon how the light reflected upon them, although strangely, the light seemed to be coming from inside the crystal balls. Some of the ribbons formed into long strings of shining pearls while others pulled out colorful bells that played the sweetest of melodies as they rocked back and forth in perfect rhythm.

The scene was indeed full of the most incredible magic that no one had ever before dreamed possible. The tree gradually lowered itself to the ground until it was firmly rooted into place and the ribbons that were once held so firmly in everyone's hands had vanished into thin air. The crowd erupted into huge cheers as the whole village had now been transformed into the most majestic of sights, with the village square being at the heart of it all.

All of the bells continued to chime as the people celebrated but after a minute they started to diminish in sound until they fell silent, except for one glass bell, on the lowest branch that had a tone that was so tender and soft on the ears but penetrated the heart. As it rang, a gentle hush fell upon the crowd as their attention was drawn to the bell.

Almost instinctually, the crowd started to part ever so slightly, as if the bell was telling them to do so, and they formed a path that opened up to one young boy in particular. The only boy who had not yet participated in the events. The very same boy who was first to taste the gift of a sweet.

In time with the chiming of the bell, he walked up to the tree. The moment he arrived at the bell it stopped chiming and a little red ribbon fell down from the clapper of the bell. After a brief pause, he reached out his hand, took hold of the ribbon and pulled so as to strike the bell. No sound came out of the bell, but the boy could see that it started vibrating, so much so that it shot millions of little lights racing through the tree. Each spine of fir was being illuminated and the tree burst into a flurry of light that rippled up from the lowest branch to the highest in just a few seconds, climaxing with a golden star bursting out of the top that glowed from within and matched the splendor of the golden gates that radiated over the village.

At the very instant the star lit up, thousands of little red robins flew out of the tree, each carrying multiple snow flakes in their beaks, dropping them one by one as they flew over the village. It really looked like it was snowing, only it was warm snow with not a single drop of it melting whether it landed on people or the ground. This was like nothing anyone had ever seen before, for this was the world's very first Christmas tree. The villagers were filled with exceeding joy and happiness so much so that they cheered as they embraced each other, dancing and singing and making merry.

Though everyone was filled with extreme excitement, from within the middle of the crowd, a man, who went unnoticed with his inside out coat, smiled a huge smile and the excitement burned most of all, deep within him. He walked over to an unnoticed table covered with a special cloth. As he removed it a sweet aroma burst throughout the town square and hundred of cups of fresh pressed hot cinnamon apple cider were exposed along with seemingly endless trays of marzipan and raisin cake, fruit pies, apple strudel, raspberry tarts, sweets, candy and divine soft chocolate truffles that melted the instant they hit the tongue.

The people couldn't hold back and once again were drawn to the table and partook to their heart's content. Every cup seemed to have just the right amount for each person and there was enough of every type of dessert so that everyone could have all they desired without there being a single scrap of food or waste left over. But the mysterious meal was not to be left without one final twist.

At the bottom of the drinking mugs there was a little message written to each person, by name, as if destiny had led them to that very cup, yet the message was the same, "Tomorrow is Christmas Day. Meet in the square for breakfast!"

Well this left a buzz of excitement that was hard for even the grumpiest of people to contain. The villagers had completely forgotten about how poor, or how cold, or how hungry they had been. Everyone was filled with excitement, and that was all that mattered.

Whereas everyone had had two of the best nights of sleep they had ever experienced, tonight was very different. With the glow from the numbers on the doors, the glimmering lights from the humongous Christmas tree that towered over the village and the anticipation of what tomorrow would bring, sleep felt like it was impossible.

Long into the night the man could hear from his house choruses of music striking up and hear neighbors knocking on neighbors' doors as the excitement built throughout the night. However, by about four in the morning everyone had fallen asleep and the man looked over the village and smiled. Snow had started to fall and the frosty ground was covered in a soft film of white that grew to a few inches deep in the breezeless night.

5. Christmas Morning

By the time morning came the whole village was aglow from the golden numbers on the houses, the array of colors that emanated from the Christmas tree and the bright reflection that the snow gave off from the rising sun, which was mostly hidden through a blanket of white shinning cloud. The Christmas tree looked astonishingly magical with the multitude of colors burning through the powdered snow that lay on top of it's branches while from underneath a deep green hue embraced the branches that gave a sense that even in the crisp harshness of an icy winter everything was still very alive at it's core.

The man had spent the first few hours before the sun came up making sure everything was properly prepared. He was very excited and though he had had no sleep he was very much awake. Tiredness didn't appear to effect him. At about thirty minutes before breakfast was to be served he blew a kiss to a very tiny bell that was just below the star at the top of the tree.

When the kiss arrived at the top of the tree the little bell started to vibrate ever so gently but enough to make the bell chime. It's little ring awoke the other bells one by one until they started to ring out the most beautiful of cheery melodies that could be heard throughout the whole village and beyond. The man couldn't contain his happiness and would spontaneously burst out into the happiest laughter and he walked back up to his house and waited and watched to see the people arrive.

The market square had never looked so inviting. The snow that lay all around was not the kind that half melts and turns sludgy when many people walk through it. Neither was it so powdery that it has no ability to stick together, and it certainly wasn't the type of freezing cold snow that makes you want to run inside after being in it for only a few minutes.

On top of the snow there was one big table that made a huge semi circle around the Christmas tree, with little gaps that allowed people to walk up to the Christmas tree. Fixed to the table were thin blocks of wood with numbers painted in shining gold. The number corresponded to the house that they lived in, one for each person who dwelt in that house. Mini bonfires were emitting enough heat that made the square feel warm, no matter where you were in it, and yet the snow still did not melt.

The villagers took their places at the table and chatted among themselves about what they thought might happen. Some were guessing what kind of breakfast awaited them, some people thought there would be more singing and story telling while others simply had no idea what awaited them. The bells on the tree played their last tune and just as they fell silent a very loud, deep and kind voice bellowed out, "Merry Christmas Everybody!" followed by a lovely, unrestrained chuckle.

Everyone looked up towards the mansion at the top of the village and saw the man walking towards them carrying an empty little brown sack over his shoulder. He was wearing a different jacket to the one he had been seen in before. This time it was made of an emerald green silk velvet, lined with a warm white material and it made his former coat look pale by comparison. He wore a matching hat and trousers, big black boots, white gloves and a hat that looked warmer than if the summertime sun was shining on him. His rosy red cheeks glowed upon his face and his smile radiated a happiness you could virtually see.

If anyone could take their gaze away from him they would have noticed that there wasn't a single face that wasn't smiling back at the man. Nobody knew his name. Nobody had spoken to him very much. Nobody had ever expected the beggar man to make everyone feel so happy.

The little boy who had been the one who dared to go up for a sweetie couldn't contain himself anymore. He jumped down from his place at the table and ran as fast as he could towards the man. The little boy's brother wasn't far behind and then as if someone had just said, "Ready, steady, go" all of the children started running towards him and gave the man a great big warm group embrace.

The adults also wanted to do the same and felt a little shy to join in, so they showed their delight at the children's unplanned reception by standing up and clapping. They didn't know why they felt that way, they just did and so they clapped and cheered while the children led the man the rest of the way to the town square.

Once they had arrived the man suggested to the children that they should return back to their families as he had a very special announcement to make.

"Ladies and gentlemen, boys and girls! Merry Christmas!" Everyone cheered and clapped again. "I want to thank you all for such a perfect welcome into your village. On the first day I arrived I was a beggar, with no shoes or coat and I came seeking for alms, and nobody gave me anything."

There was a slight moment of awkwardness, especially from the individuals who had turned him away. The people had become so quiet that you could have heard a pine needle fall from the Christmas tree if one had done so.

"I feel that it is very important for you to know that this is exactly why I chose to come to this village. I am a very fortunate man in that I have need or want of nothing except to help people find their happiness. I chose to walk here with no shoes and no coat just so I could know what it felt like to have nothing, what it felt like to be hungry and cold and what it felt like to be given nothing when I asked for it. It was exactly what I needed to feel. I knew that you had all had a very harsh year and as a village you had nothing to spare as you had only that which you needed to survive the winter.

"I also observed that you were filled with worry for your future and that worry stole joy from your lives. That is why I decided to stay around for a while. You have nothing of which to feel ashamed. I know your hearts, I know your desires and I know that you are beautiful people. The moment that you started to believe that there was something greater than what you were experiencing then you started to have hope. Only two very special little boys got to taste toffee hot chocolate candies even though I know you each wanted to try it but you first had to learn to put away some of your fear of the unknown.

"When you feasted at the table your bellies became full to your heart's content, and you were able to feel happy and motivated once again. It made you want to come and speak to me, and for that you were rewarded with a magical tree. Something that none of you could have predicted could even exist, except your hearts led you take action on your desire to know more about the great things that could appear in your future.

"You being here today shows me that you no longer fear good things happening for you. You don't only hope for great things, nor do you simply believe in great things. Your very presence means that you expect great things to come about and for having achieved that in just a few days I will not let you down. Today will be remembered as being the day you are rewarded for hoping for, believing in and taking action to ensure great things happen."

The man reached into his little, empty brown sack and it suddenly swelled in size as he pulled present after present until the Christmas tree was surrounded with gifts of all different sizes, wrapped in an array of different colors and bows that were so shiny that they looked liked they twinkled as they reflected the lights from the Christmas tree. From each bow hung a little bell and under the bell there was a small hook. The presents looked so enticing and generated excitement in the grown ups as well as the children.

Finally, the very last item he pulled from his sack was a huge chair that was as comfy as a ball of feathers yet as strong as the toughest oak. He placed it next to the presents by the Christmas tree that towered over the village and asked,

"Are you ready for a most incredible Christmas Day?"

6. A Never Ending Wish

The man smiled to the point of chuckling. He was so excited for what was about to happen. When he finally managed to contain his happiness he proceeded to give some very important instructions.

"Each of you have a number in front of you fixed to a thin piece of wood, which itself is fixed to the table. You may have noticed that it's the same number that is painted on the front of your house. I have a special gift for each of you and in order to get that gift you will need each member of your family to bring me their number, one family at a time."

Some of the children started to grab the piece of wood that had their number on it, but it was so tightly fixed to the table that it wouldn't move. Even some of the dads tried to secretly help their children but the wood simply wouldn't move.

"I might add," the man continued, "that there is a trick to getting the number off the table. All you have to do is close your eyes, and see in your mind's eye the most delicious food you want to eat for breakfast today and while you're thinking of it lift that number off the table. It's that simple! Off you go!"

Although it sounded simple it really tested the imagination. A few individuals tried to lift their number off the table while thinking of a meal, but to no avail. Once a few people had shown it was not possible to raise the numbers off the table more people started to question whether it was possible - but it only took one. One person to show what was possible and that is what happened.

The very same boy who had been given the first sweet placed his hands on his number, closed his eyes and didn't just think of a delicious breakfast. He pictured every part of his breakfast as if it was sitting there right in front of him. He remembered a picture he had once seen in a book that had stayed with him ever since he had first seen it. In his mind he saw a freshly cooked piece of bacon with a perfectly cooked runny egg inside a warm fresh baked roll, a bowl of hot honey porridge, a glass of fresh orange juice and a frothy hot chocolate made with thick sweet cream. As he pictured this in his mind he reached for his number and tried to lift it. Sure enough, it started to rise up and as it did so he opened his eyes to see.

The piece of wood was attached to four pieces of gold thread, one at each corner, going into a hole that was cut into the table. He kept lifting his number into the air and all of a sudden he started to smell fresh bacon and the scent of warm fresh bread and creamy hot chocolate. He lifted even higher and a tray started to emerge through the table. By the time it came all the way through there in front of him lay the exact breakfast he had imagined.

The tray of food rested on the table and magically the thread detached itself from the number. The boy looked up at the man in the green coat and smiled with pure joy. The man gave a huge smile back and winked a wink that didn't just say well done, but also to say I'm proud of you for being the example.

Villagers came to the boy to find out the secret. He left his breakfast on the table and went around to each family to explain how to make it happen. He told them to stop thinking about it and really try to see what they wanted in their mind as if it were already there. It wasn't long until people were closing their eyes and vividly imagining their breakfasts, lifting their numbers into the air and magically raising up their desired breakfasts with each of their names painted immaculately on the reverse side of the block of wood.

There were a few odd things that people had imagined. Someone had obviously pictured in their mind a purple chocolate frog. Another person had imagined a bowl of fruit that they invented in their mind, which they called a fuzzberry, that resembled a fluffy raspberries. One villager had even thought of eating a rainbow, which, when it appeared, made a beautiful arc over the top of their plate and tasted of seven very delicious fruits that rained down sweet syrup over vanilla strawberry waffles.

The table was soon filled with the most delicious and exotic variety of foods with such an abundance of colors that would be hard even for a great artist to imagine. Everybody ate to their heart's content and were filled to the brim with not only food and drink but also belief and awe.

When the first family had finished their food each member of the family brought their number up to the man who was now sitting in the big comfy chair. As they approached him he didn't even have to see their number but welcomed them individually by name. They gathered around him and he spoke with them lovingly about their family, what they hoped for in their futures and what they wished that they had right now.

As each person in the family shared their dreams with the kind man he gave a big smile and nodded his head, agreeing with their wishes. He then told each family member to take their board upon which the number was painted and walk around the tree, holding the boards close to the presents until the bell that hung from the bow started to chime. Once they had found it they were to turn their boards around so that the number would face the box and hang the board from the little hook under the bell.

Children and adults alike had so much fun trying to find their gift, listening for their very own bells to chime and wondering if they had wished for something different to what the man had already prepared for them. One by one, each family member would hear their bell, find their gift and turn their boards around to hang it from the hook.

In the very instant that the board was placed upon the hook the wood would turn to a fine silk and the person's name would magically appear with embroidered letters followed by the words, "May All Your Wishes Come True". It was miraculous. So much so that nobody felt rushed to tear into the present but wanted to enjoy the whole experience for as long as they could. Even for the most excitable of children it was so much fun waiting until each member of the family had found their gift before returning to their table to open their presents and discover what each person had been given.

Without exception, as each family member would open their gift they would become astounded not only at the quality of the offering they'd received but by the fact that somehow, the man had prepared for them exactly that for which they had wished.

Every family, one by one, did the same. Each time they told the man of their future hopes and dreams as well as what they wished for now. The reason he asked them for their hopes and dreams wasn't because he needed to know what they were but rather that the people needed to hear from their own mouths what their hopes and dreams were, and if he could give them a gift of something that they wanted immediately then they would likely believe that those things they had wished for in the future would also come about.

Even though he was the first to pull his board up from the table the very same boy was the last to come up to the man with his family to share his wishes, not because they were slow at eating, but because he had spent all of his time helping other people to raise their breakfasts. The young boy let his parents and brother go first and delighted in hearing what they each had to say. When it was his turn the young child thanked the man for everything that he had done for not only his family but for everyone in the village.

The man gave the young boy a huge hug, told him just how proud he was of the boy and then asked him what he wished for. The boy hesitated for a moment. He knew what he wanted to say but also knew that it would be a very big thing to ask. The man knew that the boy was wanting to get it out so he said, "Just say it young man. I think I know what it is anyway."

The young boy leaned forward and, in a quiet voice, said, "I wish there was a way that everyone in the world who wanted to could be given the same magical feeling at Christmas time."

The man gave out a beautiful laugh, not because what the boy said was funny, but because it made the man so happy that there was a little boy who thought of sharing the exciting feeling with as many people who wanted it. The young boy felt the joy that the man radiated and it made him smile almost to the point of giggling himself. After the two of them enjoyed the moment, the kind man became a little bit more serious and asked the boy,

"Do you think that it's possible for me to be everywhere at Christmas time to take presents to everyone and kindle their fires of excitement and belief in their wishes coming true?"

The little boy thought about it and replied, "I think if you had asked me last week what the taste of a toffee hot chocolate sweetie was like, I would only have imagined it but never believed it was possible. So, even though I don't quite understand how, yes, I think there could very well be a way that you could do it."

And sure enough, from that very day hundreds of years ago to this very Christmas you will find that the excitement of Christmas makes it hard to sleep all because one little boy wished all those years ago that you would feel the same excitement as the people in that very special village. But you're not the only one. Boys and girls, men and women and even dogs, cats, hamsters, bunny rabbits and all types of pets around the world go to bed at Christmas time filled with the excitement of what tomorrow will bring, that hopes and dreams are possible if only they would believe in them.

So, if you find sleeping a little difficult to do tonight then just close your eyes and think of all the things that you would like to have happen during the next year, for when you wake in the morning it will be the first day that you can start making all those wishes come true.

And if you get a present from a certain kind man who entered your house, unnoticed, then you know that someone is there for you and you can have that extra belief that your greatest desires, hopes and magnificent futures will indeed really come true.

About The Author

Once up on a time there was a beautiful mother who gave birth a baby boy and she named him, Joseph. He grew up on the Dorset coast of southern England, spending his summer days on sandy beaches, playing with his brother and three sisters and making friends with everyone. He loved to play jokes on people and always found ways to stretch his imagination to make even the hard times of life fun.

When he was four years old he started to teach himself to play the piano and a few years later he began to write his own music. Watching his brother and sister perform on stage and television Joseph thought it would be fun to start writing his own musical shows, and it wasn't long before the young teenager was clambering out of his messy bedroom at all hours of the day and night because a tune or idea suddenly popped into his head. It was a good job that he had such a patient family who rarely complained at the piano ringing out it's melodies at 4 o'clock in the morning.

Before he was no longer a teenager, Joseph had written, produced and oftentimes directed shows, commercials and even traveled all the way to London to record a television theme at a big recording studio called, Abbey Road. It wasn't long after that Joseph met the musical director at Disney who invited him to California to learn how to write music for movies. This was a dream come true for the young man who learned his trade working alongside some of the greatest composers in Hollywood.

Stretching the imagination was part of Joseph's everyday life, pushing new boundaries of music and conducting big orchestras made him feel so happy. But not completely. One day, it just so happened that he met a beautiful girl, who he fell in love with and they got married. Her name was Brooke and she also loved to create. She could paint, draw, animate on a computer and even design clothes and costumes.

Between the two of them, they had created some amazing things in their life, but nothing could quite compare to when they produced three incredible children who gave real purpose to their lives.

All the dreams, imagination and hopes that Joseph and Brooke had carried with them throughout their lives could not be contained as they started to share the very best that the world has to offer with their little ones in their own way.

However, when imagination would strike in the middle of the night Joseph learned that the pen could be just as powerful as the music he would write, only much kinder to his family when they are sleeping than the sound of a piano.

Though his pen has written several stories and novels this is the first that he decided to share with more people than just his family. And you never know… it might not be too long before you are introduced to even more characters that he's imagined than only The Christmas Man!

17674227R10037

Made in the USA
San Bernardino, CA
15 December 2014